JUN 1 8 2019

S0-AWF-898

Generously Donated By

Richard A. Freedman
Trust

the PUBLIC LIBRARY
ABQ-BERNCO

Jim Henson's™ SPLASH AND BUBBLES™

Splash's Swim School

Based on the series created by John Tartaglia
Based on the TV series teleplay written by Joe Purdy
Adaptation by Liza Charlesworth

Houghton Mifflin Harcourt
Boston   New York

3 9075 05402079 4

© 2019 The Jim Henson Company. © 2019 Herschend Studios.
JIM HENSON'S mark & logo, SPLASH AND BUBBLES mark & logo, characters,
and elements are trademarks of The Jim Henson Company. All rights reserved.
The PBS KIDS logo and PBS KIDS © PBS. Used with permission.

All rights reserved. For information about permission to reproduce selections from this book,
write to Permissions, Houghton Mifflin Harcourt Publishing Company, 3 Park Avenue,
19th Floor, New York, New York 10016.

ISBN: 978-1-328-56989-9 paper over board
ISBN: 978-1-328-56990-5 paperback

hmhco.com

Printed in China
SCP 10 9 8 7 6 5 4 3 2 1
4500749682

It was another dazzling day in Reeftown. Splash was playing with his best friends, Bubbles, Dunk, and Ripple.

Suddenly, a new group of fish swam over. All of them moved EXACTLY the same.

"Oh my goodness," said Ripple, "they all look like Splash!"

FIN FACT:
Fusiliers live in the warm tropical waters of the Indian and Pacific Oceans. They travel together in groups called schools.

"We look alike because we're all yellowback fusiliers," explained Splash. "That used to be my school!"

"Hey, Jerome!" shouted Splash to his old friend.
   "Oh, wow, Splash!" the school's leader replied.
"Say hello, everyone!"
   The school waved at EXACTLY the same time.

Splash introduced his pals to Jerome and his school.

"Hiya," said Bubbles.

"What's up?" said Dunk.

"Hello," said Ripple.

The fish friends each sounded different. They each looked different, too.

Jerome's school had been working on some new dance moves, and they wanted to show them off. "To the left, turn," Jerome said. "To the right, turn."

The fish friends were amazed. Could they dance together like the fusiliers in Jerome's school?

Splash called out, "To the left, turn. To the right, turn."

But it didn't work.

Dunk got confused and Bubbles bumped into Ripple who floated away from the group. They giggled.

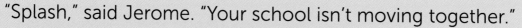

"Splash," said Jerome. "Your school isn't moving together."

   "Well, we're not actually a school. We're more of a shoal," he replied.

   "A shoal? What's that?" asked Jerome.

   "It's a group of friends that live together, but don't act exactly alike," explained Splash.

FIN FACT:
Two types of fish formations are *schools* and *shoals*. In a school, fish travel as a group for protection and to find food. A shoal is more of a social group.

Jerome asked Splash to swim off for a quiet chat.

"You're a fusilier like us," said Jerome. "Come join our school!"

Wow! Splash thought that sounded awesome. There was only one problem: Bubbles, Dunk, and Ripple were NOT invited to join.

"To be in our school, everyone has to look and act the same," Jerome explained.

No way was Splash leaving his three best buddies behind.
"Sorry, Jerome. If they can't be in the school, I can't be in it either,"
he said with a smile.

Loyal Splash returned to his friends. He had a great idea.
"Let's make our own school!" he said.
   "Like more than a shoal?" asked Ripple.
"A real school that dances together?"
   "That would be so cool!" said Bubbles.

FIN FACT:
Bubbles is a Mandarin dragonet.
Dragonets form schools. Pufferfish
and seahorses don't school, but in
Reeftown Dunk and Ripple live with
Splash and Bubbles in a shoal.

After a while, their old pal Gush came by. Gush was a purple frogfish.
   "Are you kids trying to be a school?" he asked.
   "Yup!" replied Splash. "We're practicing our dancing."

It turned out that Gush had some fancy moves of his own. He bounced up and down and did the Frogfish Flop.

"Don't give up. You'll be a school in no time!" said Gush.

Then off he swam.

Bop, roll, wiggle, waggle! Each fish friend danced in a different way. They didn't look like the fusiliers, but they *were* having a blast.

"We're all dancing how we want to dance," said Splash. That gave him a great idea.

Splash and the fish friends swam over to see Jerome and his school.
"Did you change your mind about joining us?" asked Jerome.
"No," said Splash, "but we have something to show you!"

"Presenting the Ocean Friends Forever Dancers!" said Splash. The friends took turns showing off their special moves.

"Bopping Bubbles" bopped left and right. Bop, bop!

"Rip-roaring Ripple" rolled and unrolled her tail. Roll, roll!

What fantastic dancing! Jerome and his school
were amazed. The fusiliers got so excited that they
all did a flip at EXACTLY the same time. Flippity flip!

But the show wasn't over yet. "Slam Dunk" took center stage and wiggled his tail. Wiggle, wiggle!

And "Super Splish Splash" swam sideways and waggled his fins. Waggle, waggle!

Jerome and his school loved the show. The fusiliers were
so thrilled that they all did a flop at EXACTLY the same time.
Floppity flop!

"You guys have as much school spirit as any school I've ever seen!" exclaimed Jerome.

The dance show had been a big hit. It turns out, you don't have to look or move EXACTLY alike to be great dancers . . . or great friends.

Splash suggested Jerome come up with his own special dance move—one different from all the other fusiliers.

"Well, I suppose I could give it a try," said Jerome.
He dove down and twisted around. Twist, twist!

"Go Jerome!" everyone cheered.

After that, Splash and his buddies, along with Jerome and the fusiliers, had a huge dance party. They all boogied in their own special way.

"We're one big happy school," said Splash joyfully. "Ocean Friends Forever!"